NO LONGER PROPERTY OF
Seattle Public Library

NewHolly L
JU

D1533383

IFEOMA ONYEFULU was brought up in a traditional village in
Eastern Nigeria. Her highly acclaimed children's books are renowned
for countering negative images of Africa by celebrating both its traditional
village life and its urban life. *A is for Africa*, her first book, has become
a classic title in the genre of cultural diversity and was praised by
Publishers Weekly for its 'incisive view of her country's rich heritage'.
Ifeoma has twice won the Children's Africana Book Award: Best Book for
Young Children in the USA, with *Here Comes Our Bride* and *Ikenna Goes
to Nigeria*. *Deron Goes to Nursery School* was shortlisted for the prestigious
English 4-11 Awards. Ifeoma lives in London with her two sons.

www.ifeomaonyefulu.co.uk
www.ifeomaonyefulu.co.uk/mytravels/

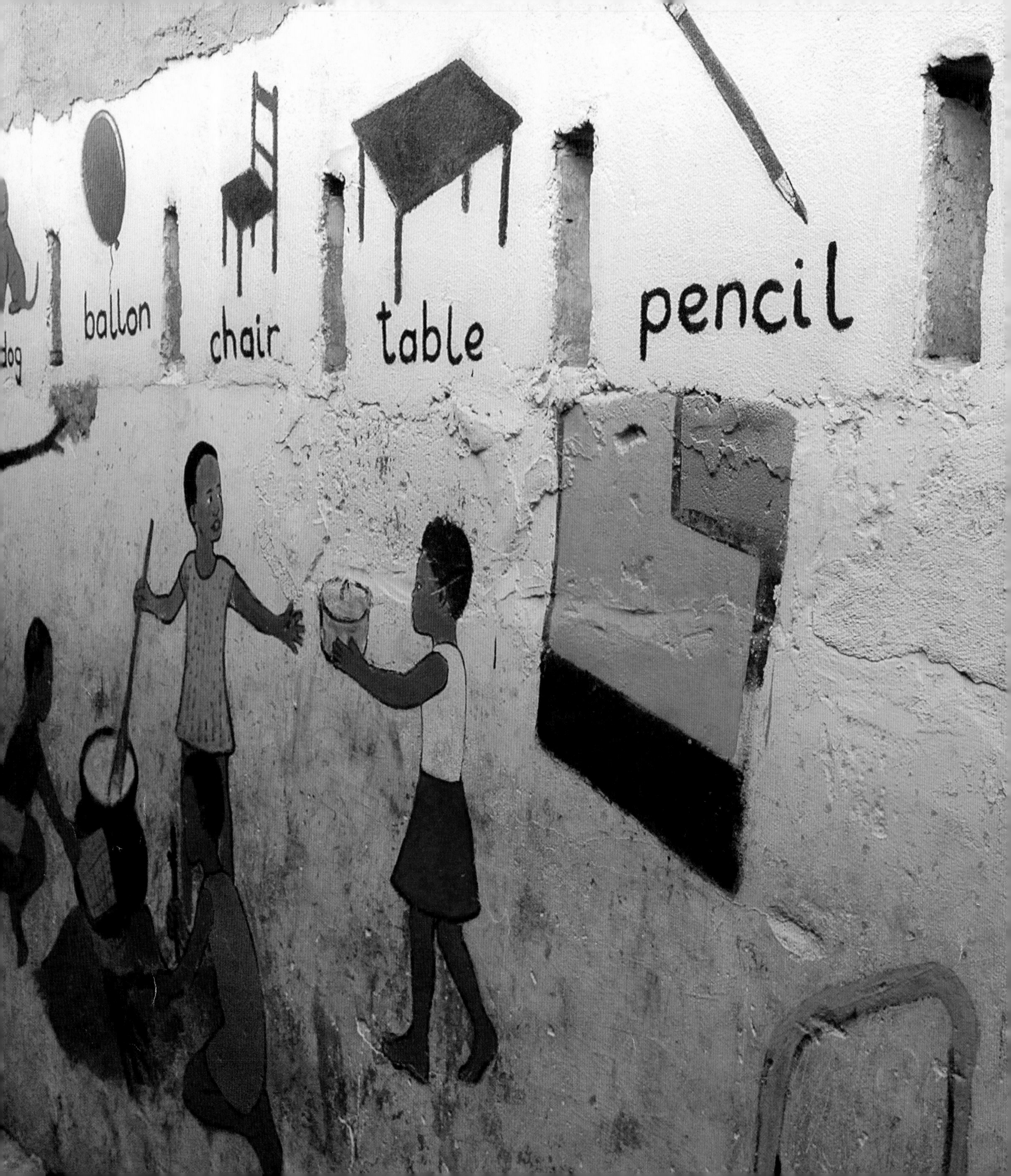
dog
ballon
chair
table
pencil

THE HOLY BIBLE

book

chalk

To Deron and the Quaye family
for their kindness and help in making this book possible

Deron Goes to Nursery School copyright © Frances Lincoln Limited 2009
Text and photographs copyright © Ifeoma Onyefulu 2009

First published in Great Britain in 2009 and the USA in 2010 by
Frances Lincoln Children's Books,
74-77 White Lion Street,
London N1 9PF
www.franceslincoln.com

This paperback edition first published in Great Britain and in the USA in 2015

All rights reserved

No part of this publication may be reproduced, stored in a retrieval system,
or transmitted, in any form, or by any means, electrical, mechanical, photocopying, recording or
otherwise without the prior written permission of the publisher or a licence permitting restricted copying.
In the United Kingdom such licences are issued by the Copyright Licensing Agency,
Saffron House, 6-10 Kirby Street, London EC1N 8TS.

A CIP catalogue record for this book is available from the British Library.

ISBN: 978-1-84780-252-1

Printed in China

1 3 5 7 9 8 6 4 2

DERON
GOES TO
NURSERY SCHOOL

Ifeoma Onyefulu

F

FRANCES LINCOLN
CHILDREN'S BOOKS

This is Deron.

Deron is four.

Deron loves playing
with his little sister Naa.

But today, Deron and Mummy
are going to the market to buy a bag...

a pair of shoes...   and some material.

Back at home, Mummy makes
Deron a shirt and a pair of shorts,
because tomorrow Deron is going
to nursery school!

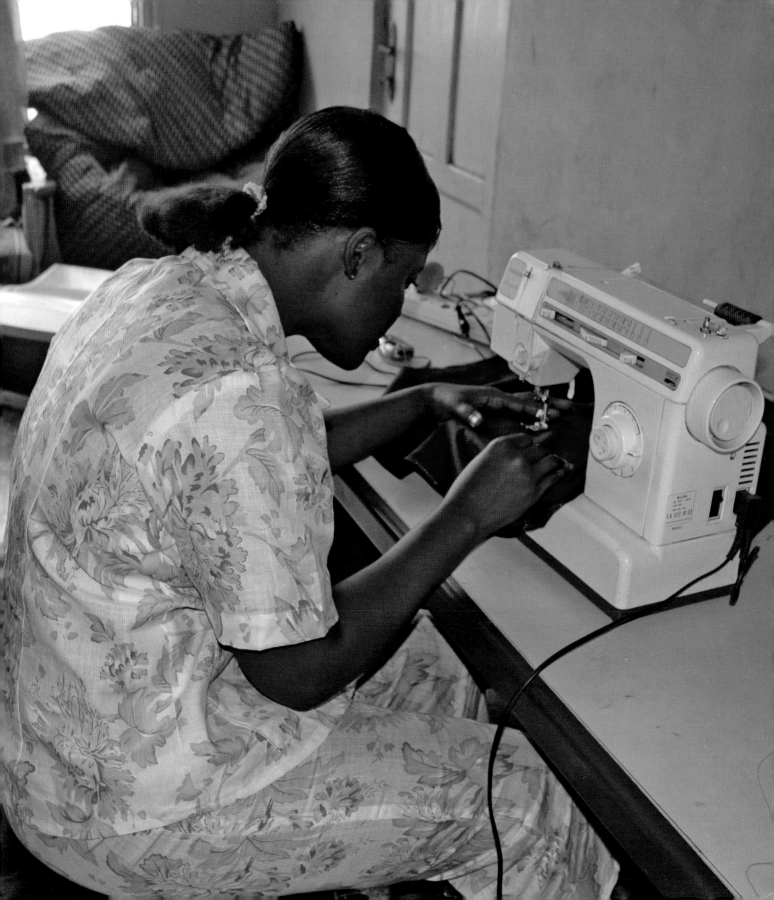

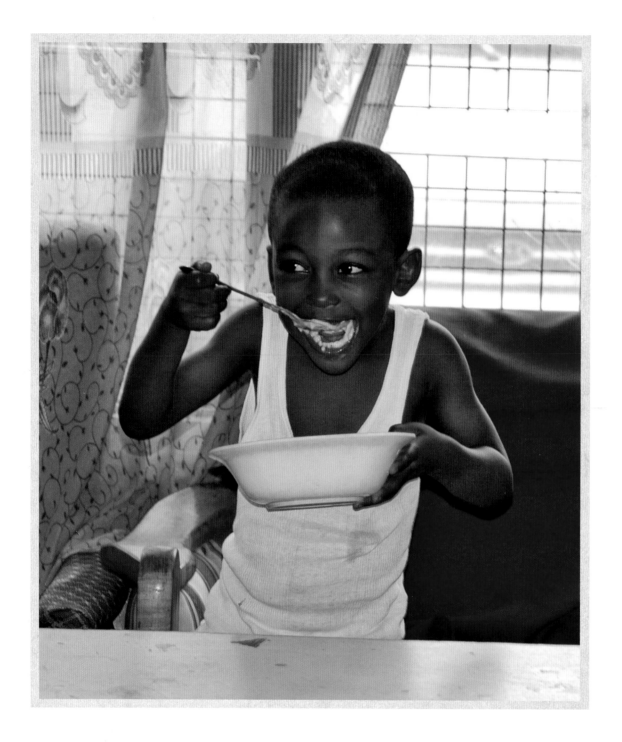

In the morning,
Deron has his breakfast.

Then Mummy helps him put on
his shoes...

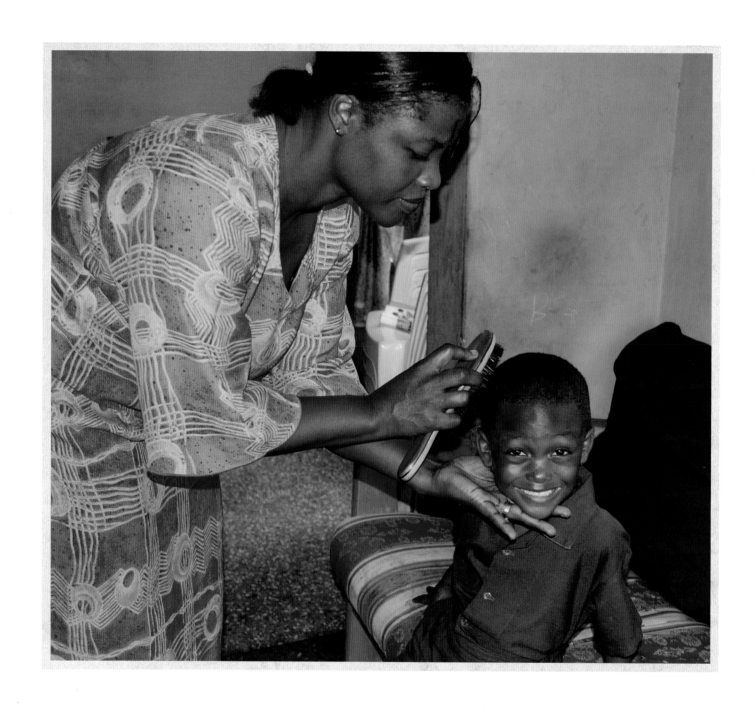

and brushes his hair.

Deron looks very smart in his new blue shirt, shorts and shoes.

And off they go to nursery school.

This is Deron's nursery school.

This is Shielabet Dadaola,
one of the teachers.

Shielabet shows Deron around...

and takes him to meet the other children.

Deron plays with them outside...

and then comes in to do a little writing.

Soon it's time for singing and dancing.

Can you spot Deron?

After that, the children play some games.

Then it's lunchtime!

After lunch, Deron makes some new friends.

Now it's time for a rest...

In the afternoon, Shielabet reads a book
to the class.

It's time to go home with Mummy.

Deron is tired. But he can't wait to play with his new friends tomorrow at nursery school!

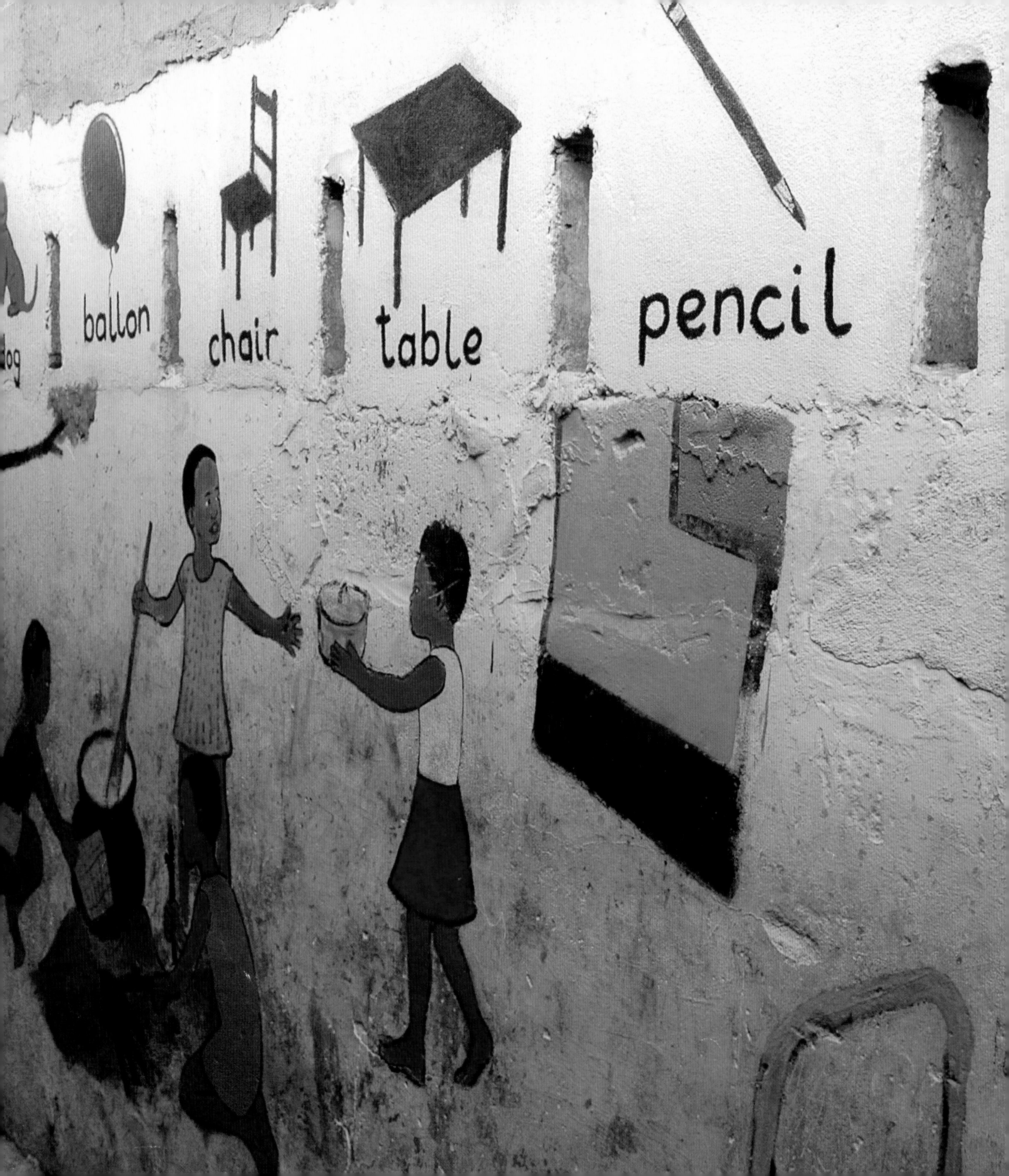
dog
ballon
chair
table
pencil

book

chalk

COLLECT ALL THE BOOKS IN IFEOMA ONYEFULU'S ACCLAIMED FIRST EXPERIENCES SERIES:

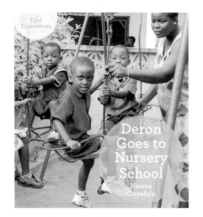

Deron Goes to Nursery School

978-1-84780-252-1

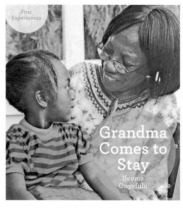

Grandma Comes to Stay

978-1-84780-251-4

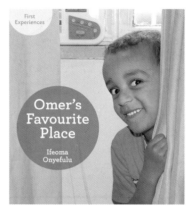

Omer's Favourite Place

978-1-84780-129-6

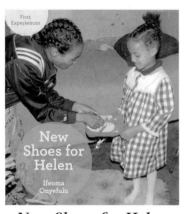

New Shoes for Helen

978-1-84780-128-9

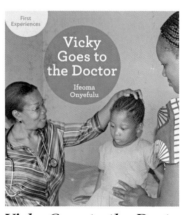

Vicky Goes to the Doctor

978-1-84780-363-4

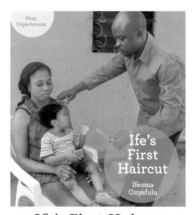

Ife's First Haircut

978-1-84780-364-1

Frances Lincoln titles are available from all good bookshops.
You can also buy books and find out more about your favourite titles, authors
and illustrators on our website: www.franceslincoln.com